A Fairy Treasure Hunt

Library of Congress Cataloging in Publication Data is available.

ISBN 978-0-545-38493-3

20 19 18 17 16 15 14 13 12 11 14 15 16 17/0

Printed in the U.S.A. 40
This edition first printing, March 2012

The Fairy Treasure Hunt

by Daisy Meadows

SCHOLASTIC INC.

The morning sun shines on Fairyland.
The Jewel Fairies are excited.
"I can't believe today is the day!" says India.

“Our Fairy Test is finally here,” Sophie agrees. “We’ve been training for so long.”

Sophie looks around the cottage at
her sisters.
They are all fairies in training.
Once they pass their Fairy Test, they
will be full fairies.

"I wonder what our challenge will be,"
Sophie says.
"There's only one way to find out,"
says Emily.

After breakfast, the fairies fly to the royal meadow.

As soon as they arrive, sparkles swirl in the sky. Queen Titania lands in front of them.

“Welcome to your Fairy Test,” the queen says.
“Your challenge will be a treasure hunt!”

“I will hide each of your jewels somewhere in Fairyland,” the queen explains.
She twirls her wand, and the seven gems magically appear.

“Believe in yourselves and help one another find the jewels,” she says.
Then the colorful gems disappear right before the fairies’ eyes.

"Find your seven jewels and you will pass the test."

The queen smiles at the young fairies.

"Soon we'll be full fairies!" Sophie whispers to herself.

"Remember, the magic is inside you," the queen says. "Good luck, Jewel Fairies!" The wise fairy twirls her wand and disappears.

“Where should we start?” Emily asks.
“She didn’t give us any clues,” Scarlett adds.

“Yes, she did,” says India. “She said the magic is inside us.”
“Maybe our magic will help us find our jewels,” says Emily.
“But how?” asks Sophie.

"Just trust your magic," says India. "Come on!"

India grabs Sophie's hand, and all the Jewel Fairies fly into the air.

Their wings sparkle in the sunlight.

"I see something!" Chloe yells with delight.
"There are golden sparkles in that tree."
Chloe dives over for a closer look.
"My jewel is hiding in a bird's nest," she says.

The fairies split up to search for the other gems.
India follows a trail of pale pink sparkles into the castle.
"My moonstone was under the queen's pillow!" she says with a giggle.

Amy and Scarlett see sparkles in the royal garden.
Scarlett finds her red jewel in the strawberry patch.
Amy's purple jewel is in a lilac bush.

Sophie searches the palace grounds, but she does not see blue sparkles anywhere.

“Look how the fountain glitters,” Lucy says.
“It must be fairy magic.”

Lucy zips down and plucks her jewel from the top of the fountain.
“Hooray!” she exclaims.

The fairies fly to the Fairyland Forest. Sophie and Emily are still looking for their gems.

Emily spies a swirl of green sparkles coming from a hole in an old log.
She peeks inside.

"Well, hello there!" Emily says to a rabbit family. "Thank you for keeping my jewel safe."
Emily gives each rabbit a pat.
Then she takes her green gem.

“We only have to find one more jewel,” Chloe says.

The fairies turn to Sophie.

“I haven’t seen blue sparkles anywhere,” Sophie says. “Maybe I don’t have any magic inside me.”

"You just need to believe in yourself," says Amy.
"What's your favorite part of being a fairy?" Scarlett asks.
Sophie thinks for a moment. "I love to make wishes come true," she says.

"Maybe you need to make your own wish now," Emily suggests.
Sophie takes a deep breath. "I'll try. Will you help me?" she asks.
The sisters nod and form a circle.

Sophie recites her wish. It sounds like a song.

“Magic might, magic may,
Be with us this very day.
In a circle fairies bow,
May magic grant my wish right now.”

The fairies touch their wands together.
A burst of blue sparkles appears.

“Look, the sparkles make a path,” India says.
The Jewel Fairies follow the trail.

“The sparkles lead through here,” says Sophie as she pushes back some leafy branches. Sophie gasps with surprise.

Queen Titania is standing in the clearing, and she has Sophie's blue jewel in her hands!

"Congratulations on finishing the treasure hunt!" the queen exclaims. "You found all the jewels. This calls for a celebration!"

Now the fairy sisters are full fairies.
The queen gives them necklaces.
Hanging from each necklace is the special jewel each fairy found.

"This has been a magical day," says India.
"Yes," Sophie agrees. "It's been like a wish come true!"